D1058162

Don't Open the Door After the Sun Goes Down

Tales of the Real and Unreal

by Al Carusone
illustrated by Andrew Glass

CLARION BOOKS • NEW YORK

Don't Open the Door After the Sun Goes Down

I'd like to express my gratitude to Nina Ignatowicz and Carol Burrell, my editors, for all their help in making this book possible. I also want to say thank you to my parents, Albert D. Carusone and Dorothy Carusone, for the twin treasures of love and reading. And finally, thanks to my wife Gwen for much more than words could ever tell.

Clarion Books
a Houghton Mifflin Company imprint
215 Park Avenue South, New York, NY 10003
Text copyright © 1994 by Albert R. Carusone
Illustrations copyright © 1994 by Andrew Glass
Illustrations executed in pencil and wash
Text is 12½-point Trump Mediaeval
Book design by Carol Goldenberg
All rights reserved.
For information about permission to reproduce selections from this book, write to Permissions, Houghton Mifflin Company, 215 Park Avenue South, New York, NY 10003.
Printed in the USA.

Library of Congress Cataloging-in-Publication Data
Carusone, Al.
    Don't open the door after the sun goes down : tales of the real and unreal / by Al Carusone ; illustrated by Andrew Glass.
        p.   cm.
    Summary: A collection of nine scary stories about a woman who is turned into a dog, a joke that makes people disappear, and other unusual situations.
    ISBN 0-395-65225-1
    1. Horror tales, American. 2. Children's stories, American
[1. Horror stories. 2. Short stories.] I. Glass, Andrew, ill.
II. Title.
PZ7.C853Do   1994
[Fic]—dc20   94-7406
                                                                CIP
                                                                AC

VB 10 9 8 7 6 5 4 3 2 1

To Kristin Hilary Carusone, Kimberly Rebecca Carusone, and Jamie Alyson Carusone, who inspired the stories in this book by uttering those magic words, "Tell us a story . . . and make it scary."

— A.C.

Contents

Don't Open the Door After the Sun Goes Down

Don't Open the Door After the Sun Goes Down

The Badoo Mountains tumbled out in front of the three backpackers like fat clouds that had grown too heavy and had come crashing down from the sky. Jarrel, the youngest and smallest of the brothers, as usual, carried the heaviest backpack. But because he was young he easily kept up with Anthony and Freddie. Ahead, the sky curdled into lumpy storm clouds. The wind whined a frosty warning.

"Blizzard coming," said Anthony. He thrust his beard, which jutted sharply from his curved jaw, into the icy wind.

"And a bad one at that," added Freddie, stroking his thin black moustache.

Jarrel was about to tell them about the weather

report he had heard on his radio before the batteries faded, but he bit his lip to stop himself from talking. Jarrel knew all too well what he would get for his efforts. Freddie would delight in cutting him down with a cruel remark. Anthony was even worse. He might cuff Jarrel alongside the face for daring to speak out. So Jarrel walked on in silence.

Up ahead, tucked into a rocky pass, stood a peculiar-looking house. It was made of the same white sandstone as the mountains around it. The front wall, however, was stained to the color of dried blood.

Anthony pushed Jarrel forward with a powerful shove. "Go and ask if we can get shelter for the night."

Jarrel climbed the three tall steps to the great metal front door. Timidly, he reached for the old-fashioned knocking ring and brought it down— once, twice, three times—onto the heavy door. Finally, with a protesting creak, the great door swung open, and a withered old man, bent over a twisted walking stick, poked a toothless face out of the shadows. "Greetings, wayfarers," he said. "Be you lost, that your path leads you to my lonely doorstep?"

Jarrel couldn't answer. His tongue lay in helpless anchor at his teeth. Pushing Jarrel aside, Anthony swaggered into the doorway. Jarrel envied the easy way Anthony took control of the situation. "Lost we are, old man," Anthony said. "Lost and hungry and in need of three warm beds."

The old man drew back his head and cocked it to one side. Jarrel thought it odd the way he looked them over from head to foot. His darting eyes seemed to be measuring them.

The old man pursed his thin lips, then opened them with a noisy pop. "I'll put the three of you up for the night," he said. "Come in. Come in."

The old man put his hand between Jarrel's shoulder blades to push him along. Jarrel hurried inside, trying to avoid the man's touch—a cold and soggy touch.

The old man ushered them upstairs. Jarrel counted thirteen steps. The third and the ninth steps squeaked under each person. The eleventh step was missing completely. At the top of the stairs was a bedroom with three sturdy beds topped with plump mattresses and thick blankets. There was a walk-in closet for stowing gear and a night stand with a candle instead of a lamp.

Jarrel studied their host as he hobbled about on his walking stick. The old man's hands were so discolored and gnarled that it was impossible to tell where the walking stick left off and the hand began.

"Do make yourselves comfortable," purred the old man in an overly friendly tone that made Jarrel suspicious.

Anthony and Freddie showed no sign of distrust. They looked overjoyed at the prospect of good warm beds and a hearty meal after their many days on the trail.

"Much thanks, kind friend," said Freddie.

"And if I might be so bold to ask," put in Anthony, "when is dinner to be served?" He gave the old man a playful slap across the shoulders in the manner of fast friends.

"In due time, in due time," said the old man. Again it seemed to Jarrel he was sizing them up with his piercing gaze.

After they were settled, the old man led them into a large dining room warmed by a fireplace that spanned an entire wall. The three brothers dug into a hearty meal of tender roast beef, fresh cheese, and crusty bread still warm from the oven.

It's odd, thought Jarrel, *the old man isn't eating*.

As though he could read Jarrel's thoughts, the old man said, "Sorry am I not to join you in your repast. But I've much work to do in my basement. For, you see, I am the coffin maker for the town in the valley below, and there has been much dying in these parts of late. My work is never done."

With this, the old man pulled himself from the table and hobbled to the basement door. "Enjoy your meal, then put yourselves to bed." His voice suddenly dropped to a wavering whisper as he added, "I have but one rule here. Whatever you should hear outside, don't answer the front door after the sun goes down."

The rule seemed an odd one to Jarrel. But he supposed that, being so far from the beaten path, the old man had to be careful at night. Anthony and Freddie didn't seem to give the matter much thought. Freddie nodded over a crumbling wedge of cheese. Anthony merely grunted and continued to cram meat and bread into his face.

When they had finished eating, Anthony turned to Freddie. "What do you say we top this meal off by draining a bottle or two of the old man's wine?"

"Sounds DE-lightful to me, dear brother," replied Freddie. "As for you, Jarrel, you can clear the table and wash the dishes."

"Yes, sir," said Jarrel, and he kept his voice steady, although he trembled inwardly at the injustice of having to do all the work.

By the time Jarrel had set the last clean dish back into the cupboard, Anthony and Freddie had already turned in for the night. Jarrel turned off the kitchen light and picked his way through the shadowy darkness to the stairway. The noisy squeak of the third step startled him. He remembered the other loose step, the ninth. It squeaked at him like a noisy fiend. Jarrel prepared to leap over the missing eleventh step when he noticed a dim light and heard the sound of hammering coming from somewhere below.

Jarrel hurried into the bedroom, careful not to awaken his brothers, lest one drunkenly toss a boot at him. The tall candle on the night stand bathed Jarrel in its friendly glow. Jarrel pulled off his jeans and shirt and put on his pajamas.

Slipping into bed, Jarrel wiggled his toes under the warm blankets. Outside, the wind howled and ice pelted the windows. In the cozy bed, Jarrel started to nod off to sleep.

.   .   .

When it happened, it happened suddenly and quite unexpectedly. A loud knocking sounded at the front door. Jarrel swung one leg over the side of the bed and was about to step onto the floor when the old man's words rang in his memory. *Whatever you should hear outside, don't answer the front door after the sun goes down.*

Jarrel jerked his leg back under the covers. He lay frozen with doubt as the knocking boomed out louder and louder. Jarrel clutched the blankets tightly to his chin and waited. At last the mound in Anthony's bed moved. Anthony tumbled out of bed, sputtering, "What is all this racket?"

Jarrel lay very still and breathed very slowly. He prayed Anthony wouldn't order him to go to the front door.

"Perhaps it's a fellow backpacker," Anthony said aloud. "I'd best let him in."

Jarrel heard his older brother pulling on his trousers. He heard Anthony curse as he struggled with his boots. Then he heard Anthony snapping his big knife onto the clasp of his belt.

Anthony's bulky shadow drifted to the stairway. Jarrel heard Anthony's clumsy jump over the missing step. Jarrel heard the squeak at the ninth step, then hushed footfalls, then the squeak at the third step. Finally, he heard the creaking of the front door. Jarrel could picture Anthony pulling it open. Then—just what did Jarrel hear? He couldn't be sure with the howling wind. Did Anthony scream? Suddenly Jarrel heard the front door crash shut, and all was as before. The storm raged outside. There was no more knocking, and there was no sound at all of Anthony.

Under the warm covers, Jarrel shivered. His goose flesh brushed against the stiff fiber of the blankets. His mind wrestled with the possibilities. Who or what had been at the front door? And what had happened to Anthony?

Gradually sleep began to overtake Jarrel. He was almost asleep when it happened again—this time a tapping at the front door. A steady tapping. With it came the gentle sobbing of a woman. Jarrel's heart went out to her. But the words of the old man sounded again in Jarrel's mind. *Whatever you should hear outside, don't answer the front door after the sun goes down.*

Jarrel heard Freddie leap out of bed and land unsteadily on the floor. He heard Freddie scramble into his clothes and fly out the bedroom door. Then came the sound of his second brother's carefree leap over the missing step. Then the squeak at the ninth step, hushed footfalls, and the squeak at the third step. Jarrel shuddered when he heard the door creak open. He heard the rush of the wind as it whooshed in. Jarrel couldn't be sure, but it sounded as if Freddie let out a piercing scream. One scream, no more. The door crashed shut.

The silence bogged down Jarrel's senses. Waves of fear swept over him. Sweat beaded out on his eyebrows. He was startled by the sound of his own teeth chattering.

Jarrel fought against sleep. But in the end, his heavy eyelids won out. He drifted into an uneasy sleep. From it, he was gradually awakened by a persistent scratching at the front door. Jarrel's eyes shot open. His ears were alive to every sound. He heard a faint mewling at the front door, the pathetic mewling of a helpless kitten.

Even in the face of the old man's warning, Jarrel could not ignore the lost kitten. He bravely sprang out of bed and pulled on his clothes.

Jarrel walked stiffly to the stairway. He was about to leap over the missing step when a sound from below made him look down into the gaping hole. In the basement, a knife lay against the wall.

"It's Anthony's knife!" Jarrel whispered in disbelief and horror.

Jarrel crept down the steps. He stepped carefully over the ninth and third steps to avoid their squeaking. Every sound he did make seemed like a shrieking siren blast to his strained senses. Even his breathing sounded too loud. And the blood pounding in his ears, surely the old man would hear that.

Once at the foot of the stairs, Jarrel steeled his mind against the mewling at the front door. *It's a trick*, he told himself, *a trick to lure me out the front door like Anthony and Freddie.*

Jarrel inched his way to the basement door. He held his breath, then slid open the door and cautiously stepped down the stone steps into the musty basement.

The basement was so gloomy that Jarrel could barely make out the old man sitting in front of a cluttered workbench. Only a dusty chandelier with but one working light bulb cast its dim light onto the old man, who sat and rocked, carving what looked like a head of cabbage with a slender knife. The single bulb glinted onto the knife as the old man hacked at the object. When the old man saw Jarrel, his face split into a terrible grin. It was all the more terrible because of the twisted black hole it left in his face, a hole that looked like nothing so much as a knothole in a board.

The old man motioned Jarrel to the workbench with the knife. When Jarrel finally saw clearly what the old man was carving, he let out a whooping scream. The old man picked up his staff and very calmly stepped toward Jarrel. Jarrel's eyes fell on Anthony's knife, leaning carelessly against the wall. He grabbed the knife and turned on the pursuing coffin maker.

A gurgle of laughter escaped the old man's wrinkled throat. "Do you really think that you can oppose me? You, a mere boy?"

Jarrel stumbled backwards a step, then another, and yet another. "What have you done to Anthony and Freddie?"

The old man held up his twisted staff. "I have turned them into wood. And you will become wood like them when my staff touches you."

Jarrel took one more step back. The rough stone wall pressed into the small of his back. A dank, wet-basement smell choked him. There was nowhere to run.

The old man advanced slowly. "Mine are very special coffins," he said. "For people do not go into my coffins. People become the wood of which my coffins are made. It is the things lurking outside my front door that dwell in my coffins." The old man laughed again, very loudly this time.

A sense of helplessness overwhelmed Jarrel. The old man lumbered toward him. Under the great chandelier beneath which he now stood, he looked more like an animated tree than a human being.

Jarrel sucked in a deep breath. He strained his muscles to raise his arm. For just a second he wobbled, his aim unsteady, then he hurled the knife at the support cord of the chandelier. For a moment the light fixture swung uncertainly. Then with a clanking it came crashing down on the terrible old man.

Jarrel turned to flee the basement. He spied an oval trap door in the wall. Pushing the door open, he stumbled out into the frosty night.

The blizzard had stopped. Big snowflakes lighted on his eyelashes and face as lazily as plump pelicans onto a glassy lake. Jarrel crossed the mountain pass and headed toward the square houses of the village below. Checkerboard patterns of light winked in warm invitation. As for the old man, Jarrel never did look under the chandelier to see if what remained was splinters or flesh and bone.

2.

Dog Days

Polli Hartaway drove along the dirt road, glancing back now and then at the long trail of dust billowing behind her red sports car. She was driving way too fast for this stretch of country road, but Polli was lost.

She thumbed through the dog-eared road map beside her. The thin line that had looked so promising as a shortcut had turned into the endless road on which Polli now sped.

"The most important meeting on my schedule," said Polli, nervously drumming her fingers on the steering wheel, "and I'm going to be late."

Then for just a moment Polli thought back to the time when her life was not a blur seen from a car window. Memories swirled through Polli's mind like snapshots tumbling in a dust storm, glimpsed only when at just the right angle.

Polli itched in her prim suit. Sweat dripped from her short-cropped hair. She was still thinking about her childhood when the big dog ambled onto the roadway.

Polli felt the thud. She swerved hard to miss the girl behind the dog. The car skidded off the road, struck a stump, and landed in a gully beside a field.

Polli jumped out of the car. "Why don't you watch where you're going!" she screamed at the girl. "Look what you did to my car."

"My dawg, you killed my dawg," sobbed the girl.

"Your dog wrecked my car," said Polli. "Take me to your home so I can get someone to pull my car out of this ditch."

The girl stared at her dog, then at Polli. Somewhere in the girl's maize-colored eyes, Polli saw dark feelings. But a curtain was quickly drawn on whatever shadows danced in the girl's mind.

The girl started across the field. "Just follow me," she said. "I'll take you where you're going."

Polli followed, hot and thirsty, under the blazing sun. She cursed whenever her high heels snagged on a root or her skirt caught on a bramble.

The girl moved effortlessly on her bare feet. Her slender legs danced through the brambles. Sometimes she glanced back at Polli, then picked up her pace. Polli struggled to keep up.

At last they reached an old farmhouse that was falling apart under the weight of its rusted metal roof. Polli stumbled up the wooden steps into a doorway without a door. Inside, a thick-waisted woman turned from the table she was setting.

Polli burst into the house. "I have to use your phone."

"We got no phone to use," said the woman. She wiped her hands slowly on the faded apron she wore.

The girl pointed at Polli. "She killed my dawg, Mama."

"That's the last straw," said Polli. "I get dragged halfway across the state to a shack that doesn't even have a phone. Now I have to listen to this brat whine about a dog that should have been on a leash."

"She was speeding, Mama," said the girl.

The older woman folded her thick arms over her waist. There was no hate in the woman's eyes. It was more like she was sizing Polli up.

"I don't have to put up with this," Polli said. "But I'll replace the dog." She slipped her wallet out of her pocket book. "What do I owe you?"

"Don't fret about that now," said the woman, pushing Polli's money away. "There's plenty of time to replace the dog." There was a soothing catch to the woman's voice as she called into the back room, "Granny, won't you please fetch some of your tonic? We have a guest."

Soon a stooped old woman shuffled into the kitchen, holding out a glass of queer-looking liquid. "Here," she said to Polli. "Drink what Granny fetched you."

Polli took the glass from the woman's wrinkled hand. She was so hot and miserable that she gulped the drink down. The tonic left a funny aftertaste in her mouth, a taste like a dog's breath.

"What about my car?" asked Polli.

"Pa and the boys can fetch it when they get home," said the girl's mother.

Polli was no longer listening. Her head felt puffy, and a numbness was spreading through her limbs. She felt so, so drowsy. It wasn't seemly or ladylike, but she kicked off her high heels and loosened her collar. Polli felt relaxed for the first time in a long while. She felt so drowsy that she lay down right on the floor, curled up, and went to sleep.

A commotion woke Polli from her sleep. Pa and the boys stomped into the house, brushing red dust from their jeans. "Well, the car's been moved," said Pa's powerful voice. He took a chewed corncob pipe from his shirt pocket and walked over to Polli. "It's good that our girl got a new dog."

Polli opened her mouth to protest, but could manage only a weak yelp.

The girl wobbled over, wearing Polli's high heels. Polli tried to get up to take the shoes away from the girl, but could only manage to get on all fours.

For a moment Polli was frightened. Then she realized that, for the first time in years, she had no place to rush to. She rolled over lazily on the floor and licked her paw.

3.

Whispered Around Lonesome Campfires

Night fell over the lofty pines like the beating wings of a great hunting owl. Its suddenness made all seven scouts, their leader, and the guide draw closer to the campfire.

The fire crackled and occasionally coughed sparks into the small circle of light in which the scouts sat cross-legged. Tom had just gotten up to stomp out a big chunk of glowing pine, when the first screech sounded from far away.

Alvie Wade turned to Tom and said matter-of-factly, "I sure hope John gets back soon. I'm starting to worry about him."

"Who's John?" Tom asked.

A couple of other scouts turned and looked at Alvie. So did Mr. Cicotta, the scout leader. Alvie, who always looked a little pale, turned two shades paler. With a nervous laugh, he said, "You kidding me or something?"

"Who's this John you're worried about?" asked Mr. Cicotta.

All the other scouts were staring at Alvie, waiting expectantly for his answer. Only Walt Klerfoot, the guide, looked away. He stood and stamped down the hard-packed ground with the heel of his boot.

"John, our senior scout," said Alvie. "Come on, you guys. A joke's a joke, but this isn't real funny."

"Tom is senior scout," said Mr. Cicotta. "You know that."

Alvie looked into the faces of the others and saw that they weren't joking. "You mean none of you remembers that John came with us?"

"Who's John?" the others repeated.

The second screech made Tom jump. It was much closer than the first.

Walt Klerfoot took a burning brand from the fire and began waving it in a distinct pattern toward the dark forest.

No one spoke for the two or three minutes Walt waved the brand, which made it seem more like two or three hours. Finally, Walt threw the brand back into the fire. A shower of tiny sparks sprayed into the air. Only when the last spark settled back into the fire did Walt break the silence.

"There is a legend about these woods," he whispered. "I heard it when I was but a boy. The funny part, though . . ."

Walt broke off and stared into the woods at some fleeting shadow.

"What's the funny part?" asked Mr. Cicotta, who was also whispering now.

Walt sat with his back to the fire. "I remember the man who told me the story. I can close my eyes and see his face. I remember our talk as though it happened yesterday."

"What's so strange about that?" asked one of the scouts.

"Not one of my people," continued Walt, "no other member of the tribe, remembers this man. It is as though he never was."

"What is the legend he told you?" asked Tom.

Walt's face darkened. For a moment it appeared he would not answer. "Once, long ago, there dwelled not far from here a man named Kittybunka," he began slowly. "Kittybunka was a great teller of jokes. The best in the world. But one day he told no more jokes. He complained that he needed solitude because he was working on the best joke ever. So Kittybunka left his village and journeyed into this forest where he devised the greatest joke of his life."

"Great," interrupted Mr. Cicotta. "I could go for a good laugh about now. What's the joke?"

"I do not know," said Walt. "No one does. For

the fates became jealous of Kittybunka and played an even bigger joke on him. Kittybunka became lost in the forest. He had his joke but no one to tell it to."

Tom whistled softly. "That would be awful for a joke teller."

Walt stood again. "The legend does not end there. The spirit of Kittybunka now roams these woods searching for victims."

"Victims?" said Tom.

"Yes, victims to hear his final joke. For, anyone who hears the joke vanishes. No trace of them remains save in the memory of one person."

"The screeches!" said Tom.

"Yes," said Walt. "The victim cries out the moment he hears the joke's end."

"Bunk," said Mr. Cicotta. "And without the Kitty in front of it."

Little more was said that night as the scouts unrolled their sleeping bags and made ready to sleep beneath the pines. A low wind had picked up at the head of the valley, and it wailed through the pines, pitching them to and fro.

Tom curled up in his bedroll, but sleep was hard coming. The story of Kittybunka filled his mind. And what of this John that Alvie Wade kept mentioning?

Despite his troubled thoughts, Tom finally drifted into a light sleep. Sometime later a rustling

beside him awoke him. He looked up groggily, not knowing what to expect.

Kneeling at Tom's shoulder was Alvie Wade. "Psst, wake up," said Alvie.

"I am awake," said Tom. "What's the matter?"

The light of the dying campfire played weakly on Alvie's face. "You've got to help me look for John. You're the only one I can turn to."

Tom's hand shot out, and he grabbed Alvie by the wrist. "No. It's too dangerous to stumble into the woods at night," Tom said. "There is no John. No Kittybunka either. Stories, just campfire stories. Go to sleep."

"I guess you're right," said Alvie. He turned toward his sleeping bag.

Tom rolled over, covered his eyes, and went back to sleep.

The sun was almost over the treetops when Tom awoke.

"Shake a leg, Tom," said Mr. Cicotta in a cheerful voice. "We've got to hustle if we want to get back on time. Scouts are punctual, you know."

Tom shook himself and rose. He rolled his sleeping bag into a tight ball and put it beside the others. Alvie Wade's sleeping bag was missing.

"Move out!" called Mr. Cicotta.

The scouts fell in behind Mr. Cicotta and Walt.

"Where's Alvie?" asked Tom. "Don't tell me he went into the woods after all."

"Who's Alvie?" asked a couple of the other scouts.

Tom opened his mouth to speak, but no words would come out.

"Move it!" cried Mr. Cicotta. "Make lively, Tom."

Tom walked on in silence. He listened intently for a screech, but he had heard nothing by the time the party reached their van and drove into town.

At the scout clubhouse everyone's family greeted them. Tom's mom and dad sat on one of the big wooden benches. His kid sister Ashley was with them. But it wasn't to them that Tom went.

Tom walked over to Alvie Wade's mother, who was standing at the edge of the street. Tom was about to speak to her when a strange look flickered across her face. "What am I doing standing here?" she said to no one in particular. "I've groceries to get."

Alvie Wade's mother nodded politely to Tom and walked off.

A hand fell on Tom's shoulder. "Want to hear a good joke, Tom?"

Tom whirled around.

Ashley smiled at him. "Want to hear it, huh?"

Tom shook his head weakly. "Think I'll pass," he said.

4.

The Stick People

Burley Rawlins was the perfect bully. Only a fifth grader, he already stood as tall as the teachers and had arms that could punch you all the way up to seven on the earthquake scale.

He was also the reason Buddy Gheen had not thanked his mother, Sara Gheen, for the new jacket she gave Buddy that morning.

It was the finest jacket Buddy had ever owned. And he knew how his widowed mother must have scrimped and saved to buy it for him. Buddy knew one other thing. The jacket would soon be the property of Burley Rawlins.

No mistake about it. Burley Rawlins would probably ask for the jacket when he took Buddy's lunch. Buddy would of course refuse. Burley would punch him and take the jacket.

Buddy glanced back along the unpaved driveway to his house. His mother was putting up the lacy curtains she had washed the night before. She smiled and waved at Buddy. He lifted a hand and listlessly waved back.

Leaves swirled over the ground. Chunks of gravel rolled under Buddy's feet as he hugged his jacket to his chest. The morning was a crisp Monday morning in October.

Soon Buddy reached the peculiar stretch of dead-end highway leading to the bus stop. The morning sun lazed in the sky. Trees, some already nude, some still dressed in autumn colors, pinched in on both sides of the little road. Ahead was the main highway. But the buzz of traffic hardly seemed real on this unused stretch of road.

Buddy was thinking of his jacket and Burley Rawlins, or he would have noticed the first shadow sifting through the treetops. The first shadow was joined by another, then another. They coiled through the tree branches like a jumble of snakes.

It was not until the thin shadows peeled themselves from the trees and gathered on the side of the road that Buddy saw them.

When the shadows began to sing in their thin voices, Buddy jumped a step backwards.

"T-the, t-the, t-the stick people are coming your

way," chanted the shadows. "T-the, t-the stick people are here to stay."

The shadows drew closer and closer to Buddy. They clumped together in some blackberry bushes. There they started taking on definite form.

The stick people. That's what they had said, and that's what they became in front of Buddy's eyes. Stick people, the kind Buddy used to draw a few years ago, stood not five feet from him. Big, ridiculously round heads. Sticks for arms and legs. Crude-looking hands and feet.

"Who are you?" asked Buddy.

"T-the, t-the, t-the stick people," came the reply. "We want what you have."

The nearest stick person walked onto the roadway. He tugged at the sleeve of Buddy's jacket. Buddy pulled away. A queer pattern of scratches covered one arm of the jacket.

More stick people pressed in on Buddy. There was menace in their spiny fingers. With a shout Buddy tore free. He ran toward the main highway.

Buddy's chest ached. The cool air sawed through his windpipe. His heart thumped against his ribs.

Buddy looked over his shoulder. The stick people had once again dissolved into a web of shadows. The shadows spilled off the road and melted into the trees. Dark shadows crisscrossed the treetops.

The stick people were chasing Buddy.

Buddy lowered his head, pumped his arms, and dashed like mad for the highway. He was almost there when an arm reached out and grabbed him.

Buddy screamed and spun around.

"What's the rush, Buddy? You wanna get to school in time to polish the teacher's apples?"

Buddy stood facing Burley Rawlins.

"The stick people wanted my jacket," said Buddy, gasping to catch his breath.

Burley looked at Buddy's jacket. "Nice jacket," he said. "Let me try it on."

Burley would have taken the jacket then and there had not the school bus squealed to a stop beside the boys. Both climbed onto the bus. Buddy sat down and looked out the window. He saw no sign of the stick people.

All the way to school, Burley Rawlins kept staring at Buddy's new jacket. The sound of Burley cracking his big knuckles filled the bus.

At school Buddy hid his jacket in his locker. He didn't take the jacket out to morning recess even though Mrs. Cavalucci protested that he would catch a cold.

As soon as recess was over, Burley demanded that Buddy open his locker. "Fork over the jacket, Gheen. Or you get a knuckle sandwich." He folded his hand, one finger at a time, into a fist the size of Buddy's head.

"It's my jacket," said Buddy.

"Correction. Was your jacket." Burley cocked the fist.

Just then Mrs. Cavalucci bustled down the hall. "Hurry, children, or you will be late for silent reading."

Buddy steadied himself and walked into the classroom. He slumped into his seat and pulled out the mystery novel he was reading.

→ Burley sprawled in his seat and yanked out the dog-eared comic book he had been reading for the past two weeks. "Now you get two, Gheen," he said, shaking his fist.

Every head in the class but one turned toward Buddy at the threat. Their eyes sparkled with a mixture of sympathy and morbid curiosity. Only Mrs. Cavalucci seemed unaware of Buddy's coming doom.

Buddy almost raised his hand to tell Mrs. Cavalucci. Almost. But to do so would forever brand him as a coward in the eyes of his classmates.

When the dismissal bell rang, Buddy almost left the jacket in his locker. Almost. But to do so would forever brand him as a coward in his own eyes.

So Buddy took the jacket from his locker under Burley's baleful glare. He slipped it on and walked to the bus. Burley followed at ten paces. The other kids parted as they walked by like a crowd scene in an old western movie. The scene just before the big gunfight.

But nothing happened until the bus dropped Buddy and Burley off at their lonely stop. Burley, who always sat by the door, got off first. Buddy walked through the silent aisle of the bus. No one looked at him. No one spoke. Mr. Tubbs, the driver, coughed impatiently to hurry Buddy along. But even he did not come up with his usual wise-crack.

Buddy stepped out, the bus pulled away, and there stood Burley Rawlins.

Burley held out his hand. He snapped his fingers. "Give it."

"No," said Buddy. "It's mine. And it's not right for you to take it."

Burley laughed while he cocked his arm. The fist shot out.

Whack!

The punch hurt, but not as bad as Buddy thought it would.

Whack came the second one. Then Burley wrestled the jacket off Buddy. "When I want something, I get it," said Burley. "If not, I fight. Then I get it anyway."

"Great rules," said Buddy. He shrugged. "Oh well, if you don't take it, the stick people will."

Burley tried on the jacket. It was too tight for

him, but that didn't stop him. "No sissies with sticks are going to horn in on my territory," he said. "Who are these clowns with the sticks?"

"You don't understand," said Buddy. "They aren't people with sticks. They're real, honest-to-goodness stick people. You know, like little kids draw."

Burley snorted. "I musta punched you silly, Buddy," he said. "Just show me these guys. I'll show them who the boss is around here." Burley thumped his chest.

Buddy pointed down the narrow roadway with a trembling finger. "Down there. But don't go. You can have the jacket."

Burley snorted again and strode down the road. Buddy hesitated, then followed at a distance.

A web of shadows started forming in the trees above Burley. But he walked on, heedless of the thrashing forms.

One by one the shadows leaped out of the trees and became stick people. The stick people rattled onto the road. Still, Burley did not stop.

The thin bodies of the stick people twisted about Burley. Buddy opened his mouth to shout, to warn Burley to run. Only a croak came out.

The stick people started dragging Burley into the blackberry bushes. But Burley fought back, punching ferociously.

Buddy ran to where the stick people and Burley

had disappeared behind the blackberry bushes. The air was still cool, but sweat stung his eyes.

The sound of Burley's punches hammered the air.

As Buddy peered into the bushes, Burley stumbled out. He was smirking in self-satisfaction. He still wore Buddy's jacket, but something looked very wrong. The jacket slumped over Burley's shoulders as though it were too big for him.

"They didn't want your dumb old jacket after all," said Burley. He slipped off the jacket and handed it to Buddy. "It don't fit."

Buddy stared at Burley's arms.

"It wasn't the jacket they were after," said Burley. "They wanted some real arms. But I fought back and took these."

Buddy stood staring at the two pencil-thin arms as Burley waved them up and down, up and down, testing them out. Buddy stared for a full minute before he started to run down the lane.

5.

The Old Woman Across the Street

Jessica saw the old woman's face across the street in the busy crowd. The face itself was not particularly frightening. It was the way the woman kept looking at Jessica that made her shiver.

The traffic light blinked to WALK, and Jessica was swept across the street by her classmates. A peculiar smell hung heavily in the air. A smell of sunshine and fresh-cut timber. As Jessica drew close to the old woman, the smell grew stronger with every step. The woman's mouth never moved, yet she spoke to Jessica. Her words were as puzzling as the disturbingly familiar smell. "Lie in the street on the morrow in the wetness of the sunshine," she said. "Do that, or you join me beyond the other sunshine." And then the old woman was gone—vanished.

Jessica grabbed Tommy Reece by the arm. "Did you see her?"

Tommy looked blankly at Jessica. "See who?"

"That old woman."

Tommy looked around. "What are you talking about?" he asked.

Jessica blinked in confusion. The smell was already fading. Jessica hurried home, wondering where she had smelled that odor before.

It was while she was doing her homework that Jessica finally remembered where she had encountered the smell before. "I'm going to go up to the attic," she told her father. "I want to look at the old rocking chair. The one with the funny smell."

Her father folded the paper crisply and set it down. "That rocking chair happened to be your great-grandmother's pride and joy," he said. "I don't think Great Gram Frieda would like you saying it stinks."

"I'm sorry," said Jessica.

Her father's eyes dimmed with sadness. "She died when I was about your age," he said.

Jessica climbed the narrow stairway and pushed open the attic door. The same smell as from the old woman curled through the dusty air.

Jessica flicked on the light and picked her way

to the battered rocking chair through heaps of boxes strewn across the floor. Thick dust covered the arms of the chair. A big cobweb hung over the back like a decorative doily.

Jessica traced her finger over one arm of the chair. With a creak of protest, it rocked. Jessica jumped.

The odd smell was very strong by the rocking chair. Beside the leg of the chair lay an overturned green bottle. Jessica picked up the bottle and held it to the light. A murky liquid clung to the sides. Jessica sniffed at the bottle. Yes, it was the same smell. She blew the layers of dust off the tattered label. SUNSHINE FURNITURE POLISH . . . SINCE 1887 was all she could make out. Jessica set the bottle back and wiped her hands across her jeans. Yes, the smell from the old woman and the bottle was the same.

Jessica headed back to the stairway more puzzled than ever. Her hand was on the light switch when she heard the rocking chair move.

Creak.

Jessica froze. The sound was an intruder to the stillness of the attic. She wondered what had made the chair move.

Creak, creak.

Jessica turned slowly. Her heart was racing like the whirling blades of a fan. She gasped. Rocking back and forth in the chair was the old woman.

The woman smiled. "Lie in the street on the morrow in the wetness of the sunshine. Or join me . . ." The old woman stretched out her hands toward Jessica.

Jessica scrambled to the attic door, lost her balance, and began to pitch down the steep stairway. She caught desperately at the railing. Only her young muscles and catlike balance saved her.

The woman in the attic had seemed so real. And the way she reached out for Jessica. That was frightening. Yet, the whole experience seemed unreal by the time Jessica rushed to her parents and blurted out, "There's an old woman in the attic who tried to kill me."

It came as no surprise to Jessica that her parents found nothing when they checked the attic. Not even the spider web draped over the back of the rocking chair had been disturbed.

"The attic is a gloomy place," Jessica's mother told her. "Your imagination took it from there. That's all there is to it."

Jessica started to her room. She hesitated, then turned back to her parents. "Do you have any pictures of Great Gram Frieda?"

Jessica's father went up into the attic again. He returned with a faded photograph. The edges were curled with age. With trembling fingers, Jessica took the photograph. It smelled faintly of the furniture polish.

The picture was that of an old woman. Down to the last wrinkle on her careworn face, it was the old woman from across the street, the old woman from the rocking chair.

The photograph slipped from Jessica's fingers to the floor where the old woman smiled up at Jessica. "Leave me alone!" Jessica screamed at the picture. "Why won't you just leave me alone?"

Jessica's father scooped up the picture and put it away without saying a word. Jessica's mother took her by the hand. "Go to bed now, you'll feel better after a good night's sleep."

Indeed, the next morning, Jessica did feel refreshed. She walked to school beneath puffy clouds, her jaw set in determination. She would not allow herself to be frightened today.

The day was normal—same squabbles with her friends, same problems with her science teacher, same boring cafeteria food. The only thing that was not quite normal was the little mix-up in her last class, gym. Somehow her towel had disappeared from her locker.

Mrs. Graham, the gym teacher, always insisted that everyone take a shower after gym. So Jessica had to wait and wait while Mrs. Graham went for a clean towel. By the time Jessica showered and left the gym, the school had emptied out.

Jessica walked through the deserted hallways to her locker. The swish of her pant legs was the only sound in the empty school. It was the silence that made Jessica think of Great Gram Frieda. Jessica ran through the halls, expecting the old woman to pop out from behind a locker at any moment.

A bell rang, and Jessica screamed.

"Don't they ever turn those things off?" Jessica wondered aloud. Then she laughed at her silly fear.

At last Jessica reached the doors. She stepped out into dazzling sunshine. Sunshine! Great Gram Frieda had said something about sunshine, something about lying in the street. Had there been another way home, Jessica would have taken it. But the clean, fresh air lifted her spirits.

Jessica ran to the intersection which would normally be swarming with her classmates. The intersection was devoid of pedestrians. A burst of traffic zoomed by, then came another burst like an instant replay. The second burst of traffic disappeared, and Jessica stood at the curb, waiting for the light to change. In the distance, tires hummed on blacktop. A bird flew out of the tree overhead. Jessica looked up at the retreating bird. When she looked down, Great Gram Frieda was standing in front of her. This time there had been no odor to warn Jessica.

"Come into the street with me. There is very little time." Great Gram Frieda grabbed Jessica and pulled her right into the middle of the street.

Tires squealed, a horn blasted, followed by a *thump, thump, thump.*

Jessica lay in the street too frightened to move. Her eyes opened and she looked into a face, but it was not the face of Great Gram Frieda. It was the bearded face of a man. "Are you hurt?" he cried. "My truck threw a tire and I lost control."

Jessica shook her head. "I'm all right. I'm lying in the wetness of the sunshine," said Jessica. "That's what she was trying to tell me." Sticky puddles of dark liquid lapped against Jessica's skin.

Jessica looked for the old woman, but she was gone. On the sidewalk where she stood a moment ago lay the overturned truck. Its wheels spun lazily, its back doors open. On the back door of the truck painted letters, all crumpled by the accident, said, SUNSHINE FURNITURE POLISH—FINE QUALITY SINCE 1887.

Jessica took a deep breath. No longer did the furniture polish smell bad to her. "Thank you, Great-grandmother," said Jessica, "for saving my life."

6.

Which Witch?

The heavy glass door of the movie theater slipped from Jeremy's fingers. As it closed with a whoosh, a shadow fell across his shoulder. He whirled to see the ticket attendant looming behind him.

"Did you miss your ride?" asked the man.

"I'm old enough to walk home alone," Jeremy said proudly. "I just wish the scary movies were in the morning," he added with a glance into the velvet warmth of the theater.

The man cracked a smile which warmed Jeremy a little. Then Jeremy turned and trailed past the dark storefronts. He sketched in the air the zigzag of streets he would follow home. There had been an unexpected rain. People from the movie roared off in cars followed by plumes of spray. Others walked along the damp sidewalk, their shoes leaving little trails of foam.

Jeremy hurried along, happy for the company of these people, who seemed less like strangers because they had seen the same movie he had.

Jeremy stopped at the corner, pulled up the collar of his jacket, looked up and down the washed-out blackness of Main Street, and crossed. Above him streetlights burned amid halos of mist; beneath him his sneakers squeaked on the damp pavement. Everything seemed to be going as it should, until Jeremy happened to look over his shoulder. The popcorn in his stomach turned into a soggy lump. A woman in a black cape topped with a witch's hood crept behind him. When Jeremy looked at her, she darted into a side street.

Fat beads of sweat popped up on Jeremy's forehead.

"I can't let the witch from the movie scare me," Jeremy said aloud. "That woman in the black cape was no witch. A lot of women have black capes like that. Even my mother does."

He approached the walls of his school penciled in inky shadow. The ivy on the walls rose and fell in the wind like a breathing chest. A screeching growl made him jump. A big black cat sprang from the ivy. "Witch's cat!" cried Jeremy.

The black cat turned to spit and hiss at an even bigger yellow cat. Jeremy laughed, but the laugh sounded thin in the darkness.

At that moment Jeremy heard the steady clicking of footsteps—footsteps that were not his own.

Jeremy slowed down. The footsteps slowed.

Jeremy walked faster. So did the footsteps.

Jeremy could not bring himself to look back. He knew the witch from the movie could not be following him. That was not possible.

Beyond the school was the church. Jeremy felt calmer as he strode past the stained-glass windows and big wooden door. But on the next block the streetlights stood far apart. Jeremy held his breath and dashed through a long patch of darkness. When he broke into a ring of light he stood panting. Warm light strummed over him, picking away the shadows like unwanted cobwebs.

A car slowed down. Jeremy froze. But the car only paused for a stop sign before speeding off. A big dog sprang from behind a holly bush. Jeremy started to run. The dog's chain jerked with a loud click. The dog barked for a moment at the end of the chain before turning back to its doghouse with an indignant sniff.

Jeremy walked on. The footsteps still shuffled behind him. But now the houses looked familiar and friendly. Jeremy had played on some of the small lawns. "Almost home," he whispered.

A light rain splashed Jeremy's face. He licked his lips. They tasted of rain and salt. Jeremy finally risked a peek over his shoulder. As though she had crept right out of the movie, the woman in the witch's cape stepped out from a shadow. Jeremy was too old to run from witches, but he lowered his head and walked as fast as his legs would go.

The witch couldn't keep up with him, but suddenly she took a shortcut through the alley. It was as though she knew just where Jeremy lived and was trying to cut him off.

Jeremy bolted down the last block to the street on which he lived. There was no sign of the witch, but he picked his way carefully up the walk to his house. The doorknob creaked in his hand as he turned it. He stood before the door, indecision making the muscles in his arm twitch, then he pushed the door open. Inside he could hear the faint clicking of footsteps.

Jeremy's skin felt hot. Should he go inside or run? He sucked in a deep breath and stepped inside his house.

In the kitchen Jeremy's mother was taking a big jar of cocoa from the cupboard. "How was the movie?" she asked.

"It wasn't all that scary," said Jeremy with a shrug. "Thanks for letting me walk home alone."

"I knew you could do it," said his mother. "But I was afraid you might get wet, so I followed you with your raincoat. Care for some hot cocoa?"

"Sure," said Jeremy. "I'll get the marshmallows." He walked over to the cupboard. On the kitchen table lay Jeremy's raincoat. Next to it was his mother's black cape, as slick as the fur of a wet cat.

7.

The Garden
of Mrs. Pottifer

When I was very young, I lived in a remote village. I don't remember its name, and I'm not even sure it had one. But I do remember the twisting road leading into the village beyond the twin hills. And I remember the little garden outside the window of my room. I remember the strange thing that happened in the garden. I remember it whenever I see a cut red rose like the kind Mrs. Pottifer used to grow in her garden.

It started on a summer day so much like any summer day.

"Say hello to Mrs. Pottifer, Bim," said my mother. I was bouncing down the four wooden steps of our little house. Across the brick street, Mrs. Pottifer worked in her garden.

"But she never answers. She just minds her plants."

"Bim." My mother squeezed my arm. "You mind your manners."

"Hello, Mrs. Pottifer," I said dutifully. The old woman didn't look up. She hovered over her plants, working with her face close to them. It was a warm morning, but she wore a yellow shawl. In it she looked like a giant bee buzzing about the garden.

"See. I told you she wouldn't answer."

My mother pushed me along. "Hush now. We've groceries to get."

We strolled along the street to the store. All the houses were brick. They looked taller than their two or three stories when I craned my head to peer at a hot-air balloon floating over town. It shimmered silver above the rooftops, and I hugged the storefronts in case the big balloon should pop like a soap bubble.

"Hello, Mrs. Mason. Hi there, Bim." It was Sundy. She was a teenager, and sometimes she was my sitter when Mother was away.

"Why hello," said my mother.

I smiled up at Sundy. Usually she had Juicy Fruit gum for me. She saw my expectant look. "Sorry, I'm fresh out of gum," she said, tousling my hair. I liked the feel of Sundy's fingers in my hair. Her own wavy red hair smelled like roses.

Suddenly Bryan Wilder was standing there. He cut between Sundy and me without a word, shoulders slouched as if he was ready for a fight.

Bryan started talking to Sundy. Spittle sprayed from his flabby lips. I couldn't understand some of the words they said. But I could tell they were arguing. Then, with a toss of her head, Sundy walked away. Bryan started after her and accidentally stepped on the big toe of my left foot.

"Oow!" I howled. But he didn't stop to say he was sorry. He ran after Sundy, still flapping his flabby lips.

Mother pulled me into Mr. Meeze's store. The big smell of fresh sausage cloaked the dozens of little smells in the store. I sniffed and picked out the hidden smells of soap, bread, dried fish, pickles, and overripe bananas.

"Good morning, Mrs. Mason," said Mr. Meeze, who greeted all his customers by name. "I made sausages this morning. I know you'll want some." Mr. Meeze was a little man with a shiny bald head. His breath was strong like coarse pepper.

My mother bought me a ten-ounce bottle of cream soda and an orange lollipop. Mr. Meeze opened the bottle of cream soda behind his counter then handed it to me with a wink.

"Oops," I said, spilling some cream soda on the floor where it beaded into a pool with a dusty cap.

Mrs. Meeze stalked over like a plump barnyard hen. She swirled a damp washcloth over the spill. "I get it, no worry. I get it," she assured me. She always carried the same yellow washcloth, tucked in the wide ribbon of her apron.

My mother bought enough groceries to fill a big bag and a small bag. I carried the small bag. When we got home, I bounded into my room to finish my cream soda and eat my lollipop while Mother stashed away groceries.

I was looking out my window, taking turns sucking on my orange lollipop and sipping cream soda, when Sundy walked up the street. Then I saw Bryan Wilder tagging along behind her.

Suddenly, Bryan grabbed Sundy and kissed her right on the lips. She spun loose and slapped him. The slap rang through the open window of my room.

"Don't ever put your slimy lips on me again, Bryan Wilder!"

"But . . ."

"You just leave me alone, do you hear? I don't ever want to see you again." With this Sundy stamped off.

Warm cream soda oozed through the gummy lollipop on my teeth. I was measuring how far I would have to spit to reach Bryan Wilder's slick-looking hair when Mrs. Pottifer walked to the edge of her garden and spoke to him.

"So that little rose wants no part of a thorn like you?" Mrs. Pottifer's voice rustled like weeds in a lashing wind.

Bryan's jaw twitched. "I'll get her, you wait and see."

"You've much to learn about wooing a fair maiden." Mrs. Pottifer crooked a finger toward her garden. "See how the flower catches the bee. Does it run about chasing the bee? No. It lures the bee with its sweet promise."

Bryan nodded. His thick lips trembled.

Mrs. Pottifer looked up and down the muscular curve of Bryan's back. "It's a fair bride you want. Well, it's a young helper I'm wanting to toil in my garden. A helper with a back as strong as a snail's shell. Follow me. Perhaps we can work something out."

They walked through the garden toward Mrs. Pottifer's house. By the time I ran out my front door, they were already in the house. I stumbled up the stony bank by the garden and wove through the nightshade bushes to a dirt-streaked window. I peered in.

"And this is the sweet fragrance which can win Sundy Jamison," Mrs. Pottifer was saying as she handed Bryan an amber vial stopped with a cork.

"Did you say a couple of drops of this perfume dabbed in the right places?" asked Bryan.

Mrs. Pottifer's face split into a grin. "Aye, a couple of drops. But don't call my potion perfume. Can mere perfume put Sundy into your hands just as easily as I can grow a red rose in my garden?"

I sucked in my breath with a low whistle. "A love potion," I whispered. Eddie Manders had often claimed that Mrs. Pottifer was a witch. The love potion that Bryan Wilder was now sliding into the small pocket above the regular pocket of his jeans proved Eddie right.

"Don't forget your part of the bargain," Mrs. Pottifer said. "You must help me in my garden."

Bryan nodded. "You promise that I'll be with Sundy?"

"Always and forever," said Mrs. Pottifer. "She is a rose that I will welcome in my garden." Once again Mrs. Pottifer looked up and down Bryan's curving spine. Bryan started for the door. I ran back to my room and hid my face in the cool pillow.

The next day I awoke to a mug of hot chocolate that my mother held out to me. "You certainly slept long enough," she said. She brushed her fingertips across my forehead. "Don't you feel well?"

Without waiting for an answer, she bustled over to the window and drew the curtains. Yellow streamers of sunlight flickered across my bed covers. The play of sunlight on my skin made me feel as cozy and warm as a loaf of fresh baked bread.

Then my mother stared out the window into Mrs. Pottifer's garden and said, "Look at the beautiful rose Mrs. Pottifer grew. Why, it's just the color of Sundy's hair."

I went to the window and peeked out. In a spot

where yesterday there was not even a rosebush, bloomed a red rose. "It does look like Sundy," I gasped.

That afternoon, Mr. Granby, the postman, brought more than mail. "Sundy Jamison is missing," he told my mother. "A search is starting this very hour."

"How terrible," said my mother. "I do hope she turns up safe."

I looked across the brick road at Mrs. Pottifer in her garden. She was stooped over the rose. I kept watch all day. I wondered if Bryan would come to work in the garden.

Later, my mother and I passed Mrs. Pottifer in her garden as we headed to Mr. Meeze's store. My mother poked me in the ribs. "Hello, Mrs. Pottifer," I said.

The old woman looked up at me for the first time ever and smiled. I could smell a musty odor seeping from the wrinkles of her skin. All she said was, "Weeds. They're everywhere. That's why I need a strong helper in my garden." Mrs. Pottifer stroked her finger across the curved shell of a snail that was crawling up the rose bush. "This is my helper. He is slow, but see how he tends my rose, always and forever."

My mother put her arm around my shoulders. "See, Bim. She talked to you."

At Mr. Meeze's store everyone buzzed with

more news. Bryan Wilder was also missing. Mr. Meeze stood on a wooden crate in the center of a group of people. "If you ask me," he said in a sure tone, "Bryan Wilder run off with Sundy, that's what happened."

A chubby man nodded in agreement. "He's been sweet on her for some time."

"Whatever would she see in that boy?" asked a woman in a green hat that sagged over her eyebrows.

On the way home, I announced to my mother in Mr. Meeze's sure tone, "If you ask me, Sundy and Bryan are trapped in Mrs. Pottifer's garden."

Her eyebrows arched, and she gave me a puzzled look that kept me from telling her about my snooping or my ideas. Instead, I started humming to myself.

We passed Mrs. Pottifer. She was yanking out weeds with swift grabs. She tossed them onto the stony bank where they shriveled under the sizzling sun.

The big snail was crawling across the rose. It lingered on each delicate petal as though planting kisses. A trail of slime traced its course. I remembered how Sundy had slapped Bryan when he grabbed her and kissed her in the street. At that moment I knew what I had to do.

Late that night I slid my feet into my bedroom slippers and padded down the stairs. The toe that

Bryan had stepped on still throbbed a little. I slipped out the front door, careful not to wake my mother, who slept on a cot downstairs since my father went away.

I stood in the cool night air with all the stars winking overhead. Then I walked into Mrs. Pottifer's garden. I didn't sneak in. I walked with shoulders held high. My penknife felt cold in the palm of my hand. The night was alive with restless sounds. Crickets chirped, moths fluttered heavily through the air, in the distance a bullfrog croaked. The damp ground of the garden sucked at my slippers as I walked to the rose. I knew what I had to do. I clipped the rose off the bush with my penknife.

Something slid against my foot. I looked down. Climbing over the toes of my slipper was the snail. With a shudder I kicked it off. It tumbled along the ground and landed upside down beneath the rosebush. I raised my foot to trample the snail, which was as big as my fist. My sore toe was hurting more than ever. "Bryan Wilder, you slimy thing. Why I ought to . . ."

But I didn't do it.

I just carried the rose home under my pajama top, pressed to my pounding heart. In my room, I set the rose into the cream soda bottle and filled the bottle with water from the bathroom.

The next day at Mr. Meeze's store, I overheard

Mr. Meeze talking to the lady with the green saggy hat. Their voices hushed into whispers when I got close. But I have good ears, and I still heard. I heard Mr. Meeze say that Mr. Granby thought he had seen Sundy and Bryan Wilder in another village.

"Run off to get married, just like I said," Mr. Meeze whispered behind his hand.

I wanted to tell them that it wasn't true. That Bryan had slimy lips. That nothing could ever make Sundy love him. I wanted to shout the truth about Mrs. Pottifer and her terrible garden. But I remembered the look my mother gave me when I tried to tell her. So I never told anyone my secret no matter how hard it tickled to get out.

8.

Dinosaur Cookies

Pudge pushed in front of Adam. He pushed in front of Mrs. O'Doole, their mother. He pushed in front of their shopping cart, which was half full of groceries and half full of empty space. Seconds ago, Pudge had filled the empty space.

Pudge began to jump up and down, pointing his finger at some odd-looking boxes just out of his reach. "Want that!" he cried.

"Mom," Adam complained, "I don't mean to complain, but this morning you bawled me out for bad manners. Now Pudge jumps off the cart like some chubby Tarzan, and you don't say boo."

Mrs. O'Doole nodded her head in weary agreement. Adam folded his arms and waited for her to scold Pudge. Instead, she said, "Well, I did promise to buy him something. Tell you what, Adam. You can have one too."

Adam shook one of the boxes down. It landed with a plop in his hands. DINOSAUR COOKIES, the box said. A TASTE OF THE PAST IN EVERY BITE.

Pudge climbed the graham crackers and was halfway up the Oreos before Mrs. O'Doole caught him around the waist and lifted him up. His hand shot by the front boxes and landed on a crumpled box in the back row.

"Mom, that box is all smashed up," said Adam. "You always say don't buy damaged goods. Make Pudge put it back."

"Want this one!" shouted Pudge, tucking the box under his arm.

Adam busied himself reading cookie labels. He didn't want to appear to be with Pudge in case Pudge dashed down the aisle with the box.

Mrs. O'Doole looked nervously at the crowd of people who had gathered about them. With a sigh, she let Pudge keep the box.

The moment they got home, Pudge tore the lid off his box of cookies. Before he could eat one, Mrs. O'Doole snatched the box away and set it on the top shelf of the pantry. "Not until after dinner," she admonished him. "You'll spoil your appetite."

Adam set his box next to Pudge's. That was when Pudge's box wiggled—ever so slightly. "Pudge's dinosaur cookies wiggled all by themselves," said Adam. "That's what he gets for picking a damaged box. It probably has cookie worms in it."

Mrs. O'Doole picked up the damaged box by one corner and gingerly deposited it into the trash. "I'm sure Adam will share his dinosaur cookies with you, Pudge," she said with a hopeful smile.

"I will not," sputtered Adam. "I told him not to get that box."

"We can discuss it after you do your homework," Mrs. O'Doole said.

After dinner, Adam started his math homework. It was one of those nights when the pencil dragged across every problem. Pudge didn't help matters any. He stood in front of the television set, flapping his arms and repeating everything that Big Bird said. Big Bird was Pudge's hero. Pudge looked a lot like his hero, thought Adam. In fact, if Pudge had yellow feathers, they might pass for twins.

Finally, Adam got to the last problem. He stood up. "I'm going to the bathroom," he told Pudge. "Don't so much as breathe on my homework."

When Adam returned, his math homework was nowhere in sight. "Where is it, Pudge?" shouted Adam.

Pudge held out both hands, palms up. "Pudge don't have."

Adam frantically searched the room. He lifted

sofa cushions, shook curtains, and peered under chairs. All the while Pudge squatted in front of the television chirping like a bird.

"What's that you're sitting on?" asked Adam.

"My nest," said Pudge with a satisfied smile. "I'm a birdie."

Adam pushed Pudge off the nest. Shredded strips of paper lined Pudge's favorite cookie bowl.

"My homework!" shouted Adam. He grabbed Pudge by the hair. "I know one birdie who's going to get plucked."

Mrs. O'Doole rushed into the room. "Adam, don't pick on your brother," she said. "You should know better than to leave your homework unattended."

As Adam redid his math homework, he plotted to get even with Pudge. Pudge was big on doing everything first. So Adam casually stood up. Everything had to be done just right to pull off his plan. He stretched and yawned. "I think I'll brush my teeth," he said in a matter-of-fact tone.

Pudge flew off like a real bird. He tore into the bathroom and stomped back out wearing a toothpaste moustache. "Pudge brush first," he announced proudly to Adam. He waved one finger in the air. "Pudge number one."

"You know the rules," said Adam with a smile. "No snacks after brushing. Too bad, Pudgie bird, you can't have a snack of dinosaur cookies."

Pudge began screaming and making such a ruckus that Adam was afraid their mother would break the no-snacks-after-brushing rule. She didn't, but she did something just as bad. "You brush too, Adam," she said. "You can both have the dinosaur cookies tomorrow."

Adam stomped into the bathroom. He jammed his toothbrush into his mouth and rattled it over his teeth. Then he stomped into the bedroom. Pudge waddled after him.

When Pudge said goodnight, Adam glared at him without speaking. Pudge had a sneaky look in his eyes.

Adam kept a wary eye on Pudge as long as he could, but finally he drifted off to sleep. Then, in the dead of the night, Adam woke up to a chomp, chomp, chomping noise. The sound shattered the stillness.

"Ho, ho," said Adam. "I'll bet Pudge is eating my dinosaur cookies."

Adam rolled out of bed and headed for the kitchen. From behind the pantry door came the sounds of munching. The sound of cookies being munched.

Adam grabbed the doorknob and started to turn it when he thought he heard Pudge calling him from the bedroom.

Adam's hand slipped off the doorknob. If Pudge was in the bedroom, who—or what—was in the pantry eating cookies? Adam steadied himself, grabbed the doorknob, and pushed open the pantry door.

A box of dinosaur cookies lay mangled on the floor. Adam picked up the box and shook it. Only a few tiny crumbs fell out.

Just then the basement door squeaked open. Adam heard footfalls creaking down the basement steps. He ran to the basement door. "Pudge," he called out. "Are you down there?"

There was no answer. Adam flipped on the light and ventured down the first three steps.

From deep within the basement, came the loud munching sounds that Adam had heard before. His legs began to feel wobbly, but Adam steadied them and walked down the remaining steps. Fog stung his eyes. With each step he felt like he was walking back further and further in time.

Adam stopped at the bottom of the steps to peer around the basement. As he did so, the light went out. The door above him slammed shut and the lock clicked into place. "Hide and seek," came Pudge's cheerful voice.

Something moved against the wall. Adam sucked in his breath. Heavy footsteps. A swishing sound like a long tail whipping back and forth.

Adam stumbled through the darkness, groping his way back to the steps. The thing started thumping along after him.

Adam scurried up the steps on his hands and feet. The thing groaned behind him. It reached the first step. The step snapped and splintered with a crackling sound. Step after step came crashing down behind Adam. But he reached the top first. He pounded on the door. "Let me out!" he screamed as hot breath sprayed onto the back of his head.

The door flew open. "What is going on?" said Adam's mother, standing in the doorway. Suddenly her eyes grew big. "Run!" she shouted, pointing to the thing behind Adam.

Adam was halfway through the kitchen when Pudge scooted past him, going toward the thing.

Adam turned around. A giant dinosaur cookie towered over Pudge. It lashed its tail against the refrigerator. Its head bumped the ceiling.

Pudge stood directly under the giant cookie. Pudge had a big spoon in one hand, and clutched in the other hand was Pudge's favorite cookie bowl.

"Save Pudge," Mrs. O'Doole cried. "He doesn't stand a chance."

But in the end it was the dinosaur cookie that didn't stand a chance. Pudge did what Pudge did best. He ate and ate. "Milk!" he demanded, pounding his spoon on the table.

Mrs. O'Doole pulled a gallon container of milk from the refrigerator and handed it to Pudge. Pudge ate and drank. He ate so much dinosaur cookie

that Adam's stomach began to ache just watching him.

Adam held his stomach and moaned. He rolled out of bed still holding his stomach. "A dream," said Adam. "It was just a dream." And he made up his mind right then and there that he would let Pudge have all the dinosaur cookies he wanted.

9.

The Crying Dollhouse

Jodi knew she had to have the dollhouse as soon as she saw it. It had turrets and gables, a wide porch and a hanging swing, and tucked into the deepest corner of the biggest room was a fireplace. It was just the sort of fireplace Jodi's father was always talking about having someday in a real house. It was the kind of fireplace you could sit in front of and toast marshmallows while you warmed your hands after coming in from the snow.

Jodi padded timidly toward the woman behind the counter at the dollhouse store. The woman was reading a book. Jodi thought she would politely ask her how much the dollhouse cost, and that would be that. Of course the dollhouse would be much too expensive for Jodi. But she had to ask.

Jodi cleared her throat, and the woman looked up at her.

"Excuse me, but how much is that dollhouse?" Jodi asked.

The woman wore a purple headband, giving her the look of someone planning to burst into an aerobics routine at any second. However, she calmly set the book down. "I was reading about ghosts," she said with a smile. "Fascinating subject, ghosts. Do you know anything about ghosts, young lady?"

"Not much," Jodi admitted.

The woman frowned like a schoolteacher receiving a wrong answer in class. "Not many people do," she said. "And what little they think they know is pure hogwash passed down from generation to generation."

"I see," said Jodi, shuffling her feet impatiently and very much wanting to turn the subject back to dollhouses.

"For example," the woman said, adjusting her purple headband rakishly over one eye. "Not many people realize what a sacrifice a ghost must make to come back to haunt, let's say, a house. Because if a ghost does choose to come here, there is positively no guarantee she will ever get back *there*."

"Get back where?" Jodi asked.

"To the place where it is possible to think two thoughts at once," replied the woman. "Have you ever tried to think two thoughts at once?"

"No," admitted Jodi. "That seems awfully hard to do."

"Not for a ghost," replied the woman. "Unless that ghost just happened to come here. Then it's hard enough to think just one thought at a time, what with all the bustle and confusion. So a ghost has to have a pretty good reason for coming here. Either that, or be of the twisted sort, if you gather my meaning." With this the woman twisted the purple headband over one ear.

Jodi stared openmouthed at the woman. She had not expected to learn quite so much about ghosts while shopping for a dollhouse. The two subjects seemed very far removed.

The woman suddenly vaulted onto the counter in front of her and sat there cross-legged with her arms folded across her chest. "Getting back to your original question about the price of the dollhouse, let me contemplate," she said. And she scrunched her eyes shut and began to hum in a most contemplative drone.

As the minutes dragged on, Jodi began to fear that the woman had gone into some sort of trance and would never answer her question. At least, she wouldn't answer it in the fifteen minutes which Jodi's mother had, in no uncertain terms, allotted Jodi to look around in the store. Jodi edged back to the dollhouse and checked for a price tag. All the while she kept one wary eye on the humming woman and the other on the parking lot, where her mother might start impatiently tooting the car horn at any moment.

In the race to see which would happen first, the woman with the purple headband won. Her eyes, which were shadowed the same shade of purple as the headband, shot open. "The price of the dollhouse all depends," said the woman.

"Depends on what?" asked Jodi. "I thought a price was a price."

"A price is a price," said the woman. "But this particular price depends on three things. First of all, what is your name?"

Jodi, who thought that a person's name had nothing to do with a price, nevertheless answered, "Jodi Daniels."

"Ah, good," said the woman, and with her finger she drew an imaginary check mark in the air like a teacher checking off a correct answer on a test paper. "Now for the second question. Are your parents Curt and Karen Daniels, and are they planning to move soon?"

"How could you know that?" Jodi asked, stumbling back a step.

"I'll ask the questions here," the woman said. "Your job is to supply the answers."

Jodi nodded dumbly.

"That's two correct answers," the woman said. She uncrossed her legs and began pedaling the air furiously, as though riding an upside-down bicycle. "Now for the final question," she said. "How much money do you have?"

Jodi's hand crept into her pocket to stroke the roll of money she had saved from her allowance and her birthday. "One hundred twenty-two dollars and eighty-five cents," she said with a sigh.

The woman hopped down from the counter and wiped her brow. "I don't get much *physical* activity," she said between puffs. "So I like to squeeze in all I can while I've got the chance."

Jodi, who had the impression that the weird woman did not get out much, asked, "How much is the dollhouse?"

"It's exactly one hundred twenty-two dollars and eighty-three cents."

Jodi broke into a big smile just as the first blast of the car horn pierced the quiet of the little shop. Hurriedly, she placed her money on the counter.

"There is one catch," the woman said. "I don't have the two cents for your change. Will you trust me to make up the difference?"

Jodi waved her hand with a carefree flick of the wrist. "Forget the change."

"Oh no, I always even the score," the woman said in a most peculiar tone. "Even if it takes a very, very long time."

Just then the car horn blared again, much more insistently this time. The woman helped Jodi carry the dollhouse to the station wagon where Jodi's mother sat impatiently drumming her fingers on the steering wheel.

Jodi opened the back gate of the station wagon. The woman pushed the dollhouse securely in.

"Wow!" said Jodi's mother. "It's gorgeous, but the deal was you couldn't spend more than you had saved. You know that, Jodi."

"It's all taken care of," said the woman. "I hope it's everything that you want."

It was what Jodi wanted, but what happened that first night was not what she wanted at all. It was downright frightening. Jodi had set the dollhouse up in the corner of her room. She moved her doll family into the spacious house and posed them around the fireplace.

"Time for bed," Jodi's mother called out.

"We want you rested to help with the packing," added her father, coming to Jodi's door. "Because in a couple of days, we are moving into our very own house."

"I thought we had agreed to wait until tomorrow to tell Jodi," said Jodi's mother. "Now she won't sleep a wink."

Jodi's father covered his mouth with his hand. His eyes twinkled merrily as he made like a ventriloquist and spoke without moving his lips. "I won't say another word on the subject. Well, maybe just one more word. And that word is fireplace."

Jodi clapped her hands together and squealed in delight. "Just like we always wanted. Now we'll be just like my doll family."

Jodi drifted into sleep wondering what the new house would be like. She was sleeping peacefully when the sound of crying woke her. At first, Jodi thought she had been dreaming. Then the crying started up again. It was so strange. The crying stretched over the room like a skin stretching over cooling pudding. It was just a thin wail at first, a pitiful little voice crying in the night.

Jodi sat bolt upright in her bed. The distorted shapes and sizes of night seemed to be reaching for her, running their wispy fingers through her hair. Jodi shivered and pulled the bed sheets tightly to her neck.

The sound of another crying voice suddenly joined the first. Whereas the first voice was that of a child, this was the voice of a woman. Finally a third voice chimed in. It was the voice of a man.

The hands of the wall clock dragged themselves along their circular path as the crying went on and on. Ten minutes passed before Jodi could bring herself to slide out of bed. Her first impulse was to run to her parents' room, but the crying no longer scared her now. It was sad, woefully sad, as though all hope and happiness had been drained from the voices that uttered it.

Jodi walked to the window, for common sense told her that was where the crying was coming from. She threw open the window. But outside were only the sounds of the night and the faraway drone of traffic on the highway.

Inside, the symphony of crying voices swelled and filled the room. Jodi turned and carefully searched her room, looking for the source. She did not flick the light on. Somehow, she felt instinctively that the crying would wither and fade in the sudden glare of the light, vanish as shadows do.

Step by step, Jodi pursued the elusive voices. And each step brought her closer to her dollhouse. Jodi realized the crying was coming from inside the dollhouse. She stooped and peered into the tiny windows. The sound of crying swirled about the doll house, thick as mist.

And then Jodi froze. Inside the dollhouse, Jodi's dolls floated about the fireplace. At first Jodi thought they were dancing. But she soon realized they were caught up in some amazing draft that

existed only in the dollhouse. And it was the three dolls who were crying.

Jodi stared in disbelief at the floating dolls, the mother doll, the father doll, and the daughter doll. The faces of the dolls were no longer the egg smooth, blank faces they had been. They now had lines etched with feeling and expression just like real people. And the dolls looked hauntingly familiar. Jodi trembled as she realized the faces of the dolls were the faces of her own family.

Then a fourth figure seeped into the room, seeped right through the walls and joined the others. This figure was different from the others. It looked transparent, like a floating ball of gases—like a ghost. Its face was disturbingly familiar. It wore a purple headband.

The ghost doll in the purple headband began to shriek at the other dolls. It drove them toward the fireplace. The crying dolls were pushed into the fireplace and were sucked up the chimney like smoke. Their crying turned into bone-chilling screams.

Jodi screamed too.

She rushed out from the room and hammered on her parents' door.

"What's the matter?" asked her father.

"My new dollhouse," gasped Jodi. "It turned my dolls into us and made them cry. Then the ghost in the purple headband pushed us into the fire-place."

"Whoa there, slow down," said Jodi's mother, throwing a comforting arm over Jodi's shoulders. "Sounds like you had a nightmare, that's all."

"Come, we'll check out the dollhouse with you," said Jodi's father.

"No, I won't go near it!" Jodi screamed. She pulled away from her mother.

"Listen to yourself, Jodi," her father said. "You're letting your imagination run wild."

"It's best to confront your fears," her mother said in a gentle voice.

And so Jodi went back into her room, sand-wiched between her mother and father. The vision of those three screaming dolls that looked like her family swirled about Jodi's head. And that ghost doll with the purple headband, it was the scariest of all.

Jodi's father turned on the light. Jodi squeezed her eyes shut, waiting for her parents to gasp at the horrible sight. But nothing happened. Jodi opened her eyes. The dollhouse lay quiet and empty.

"See, there's nothing to worry about," said Jodi's mother. "It was all just a dream."

"What's this?" asked her father as he picked up three charred black lumps from the floor by the dollhouse. "Looks like melted plastic."

Jodi threw open the door of the dollhouse. "My dolls are gone," she cried. "It wasn't a dream."

They searched around the dollhouse, but there was no sign of the dolls.

"Where could they be?" asked Jodi as she rolled the charred lumps over and over in her hand.

Her father shrugged his shoulders. He agreed to take the dollhouse out to the garage. And so, at a quarter to three in the morning, he toted the dollhouse to the garage and set it among the oily rags and piles of sawdust on his workbench.

The next day, Jodi's mother drove her back to the little store to return the dollhouse to the woman in the purple headband.

"It's gone," Jodi said, staring at the empty building. "There's no store here."

"Doesn't surprise me one bit," said her mother. "Selling dollhouses that frighten children. No wonder they're out of business."

They returned the dollhouse to the garage, where it was forgotten as the excitement of moving swept over them.

They drove to the new house ahead of the moving van. The real estate agent, Miss Combs, met them at the door with a big bundle of papers. "It's all yours now," she said. "Signed, sealed, and delivered." With a sweeping bow, she led them into the house.

From the outside, the house had not been

remarkable. It was in need of a fresh coat of paint, and it was not much bigger than the rented house they had left behind. But the inside was perfectly preserved.

As Jodi walked through the house, the strangest feeling swept over her. Jodi could not shake the feeling that she had been in this house before. But that was not possible. It was only as they walked into the big room with the fireplace that the truth dawned eerily on Jodi. Jodi had not been inside this house before. But she *had* seen these rooms before. They were the rooms of the dollhouse.

Jodi's parents stood before the fireplace, admiring it. And suddenly Jodi realized they were standing in exactly the same positions as Jodi had placed her dolls. Jodi searched the face of Miss Combs, almost expecting her to change into the woman with the purple headband. But she did not. Then Jodi saw the picture hanging on the wall. Her breath shot from her chest like aerosol spray.

The picture was a portrait of the woman at the doll shop, minus her purple headband. "Who is that?" Jodi blurted out to the real estate agent.

"Elvita Curringer," Miss Combs answered with a pleasant smile. "She was the original owner of this house."

"Where is she now?" Jodi asked.

"Why, she's been dead for almost sixty years," said Miss Combs.

Jodi's mother muttered something about the beauty of the portrait, but she gave no sign of recognizing the woman.

Jodi's father quickly lost interest in the portrait. "I'll just mosey on over to the fireplace," he said. "I've always wanted a fireplace. We'll have a nice big fire tonight, whether it's warm or cool."

"Don't go near the fireplace," Jodi shouted. She threw herself in front of her father to stop him, fearing he would somehow be sucked up the chimney.

They both crashed into the fireplace.

Loose mortar fell from the flue like snowfall. Her father helped Jodi up, then peered intently up the chimney. He whistled softly. "You were right to fear this fireplace," he said to Jodi. "The weight of our bodies was enough to disclose the weakness of the mortar. One fire in this fireplace would have been our last."

"I'll get it repaired at once." Miss Combs tittered nervously.

At that moment, a purple headband fell down the chimney. It landed with a rustle in the fireplace. Two charred black objects plunked down beside the headband.

Jodi picked up the charred objects.

"What are they?" asked her mother.

"Two very old pennies," said Jodi, showing

them to her mother. Jodi smiled at the portrait on the wall. "They're my change."

The purple headband, Jodi kept always. The two pennies she cast into a wishing well and wished with all her heart that the woman who once wore the purple headband might get back to the place where it was possible to think two thoughts at once.

About the Author and Illustrator

Al Carusone has been a nuclear reactor operator, an ice cream maker, and a junior high school teacher, and is now busy developing weather programs for earth science classes. He received a B.S. in Geology and an M.A. in Teaching from the University of Pittsburgh. Mr. Carusone lives in Howard, Pennsylvania, with his wife and three daughters. *Don't Open the Door After the Sun Goes Down* is his first book for children.

Andrew Glass has illustrated many picture books, some of which he wrote himself. He has recently done jacket and interior illustrations for two other Clarion novels, David Gifaldi's *Gregory, Maw, and the Mean One* and Susan Mathias Smith's *The Booford Summer*. Mr. Glass lives in New York City.